THIS WALKER BOOK BELONGS TO:

_____

_____

_____

_____

This book is dedicated to
Eliza Garwood, Jessica Lawrence
and BEAR with all my love

First published 1999 by Walker Books Ltd
87 Vauxhall Walk, London SE11 5HJ

2 4 6 8 10 9 7 5 3

© 1999 Naomi Russell

This book has been typeset in Goudy.

Printed in Hong Kong

British Library Cataloguing in Publication Data
A catalogue record for this book is
available from the British Library.

ISBN 0-7445-3988-9

Who's in the Jungle?

Naomi Russell

WALKER BOOKS
AND SUBSIDIARIES
LONDON • BOSTON • SYDNEY

Who's squawking
in the leaves?

The parrot!

Who's splashing
in the river?

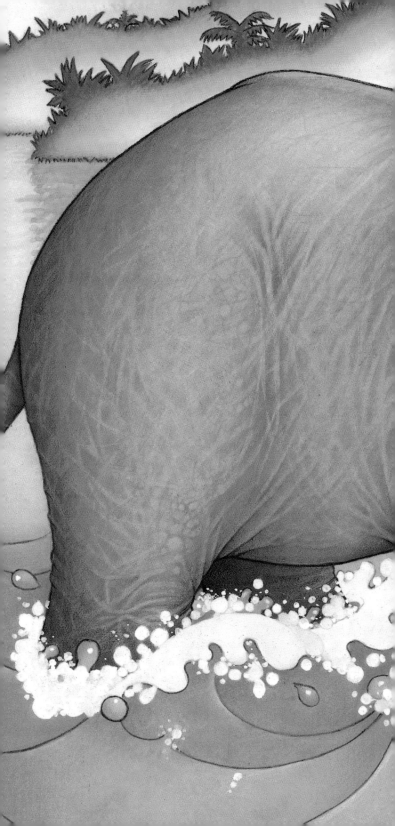

The elephant!

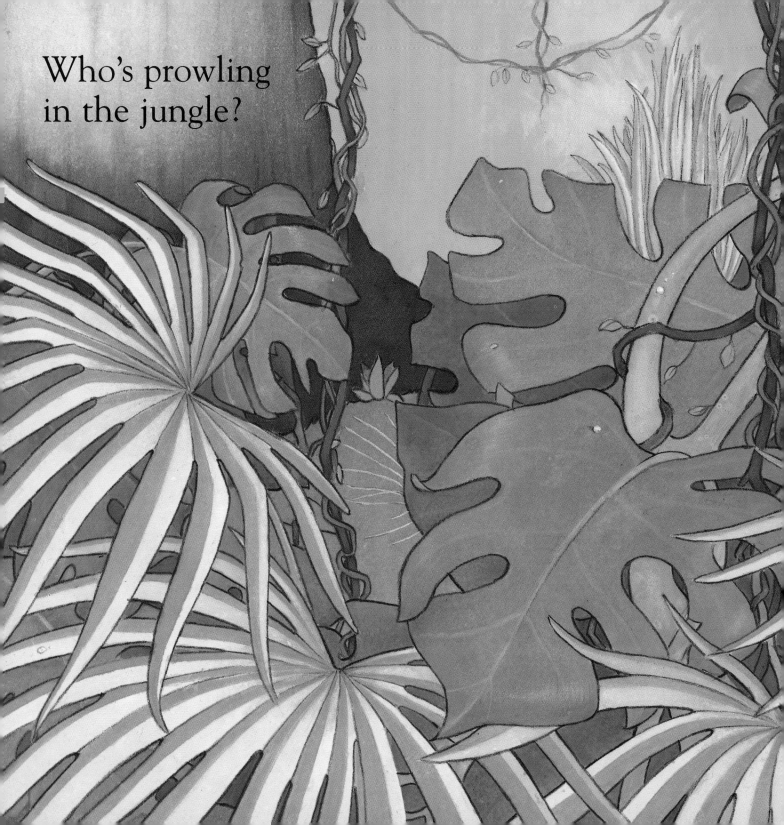

Who's prowling
in the jungle?

The tiger!

Who's hissing
in the branches?

The snake!

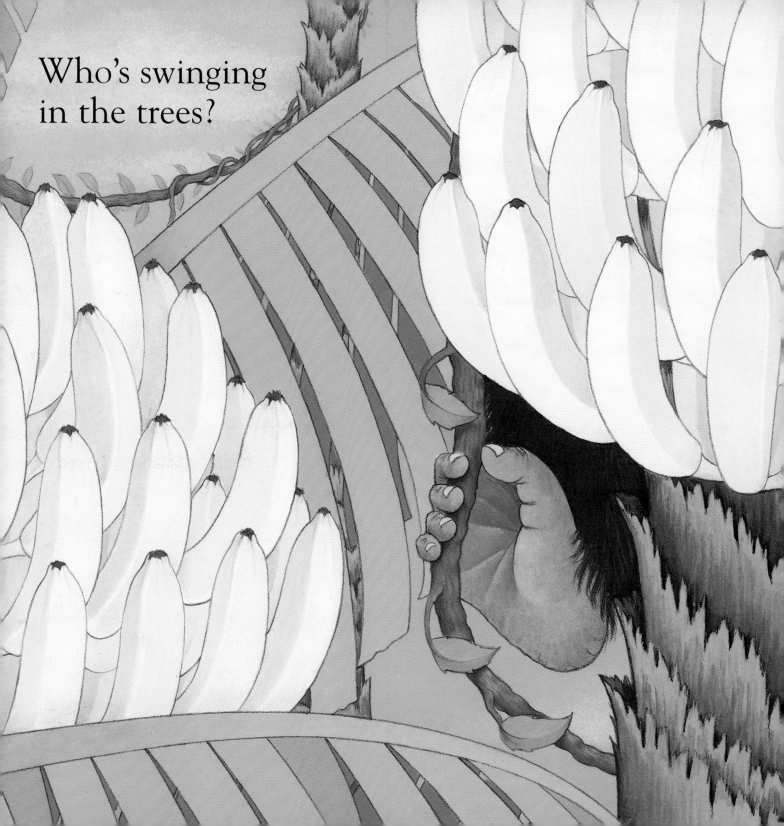

Who's swinging
in the trees?

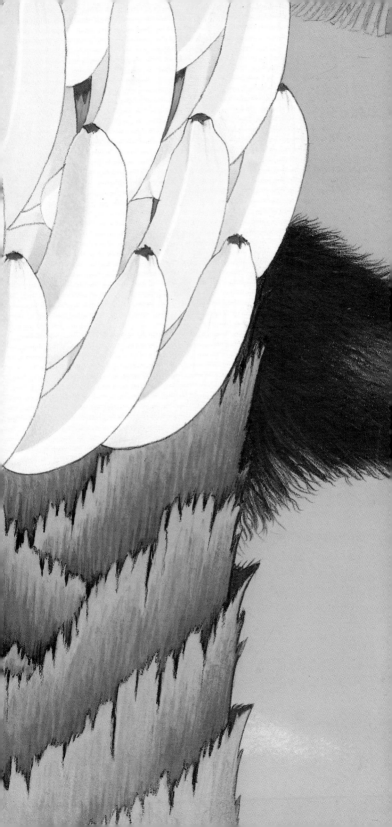

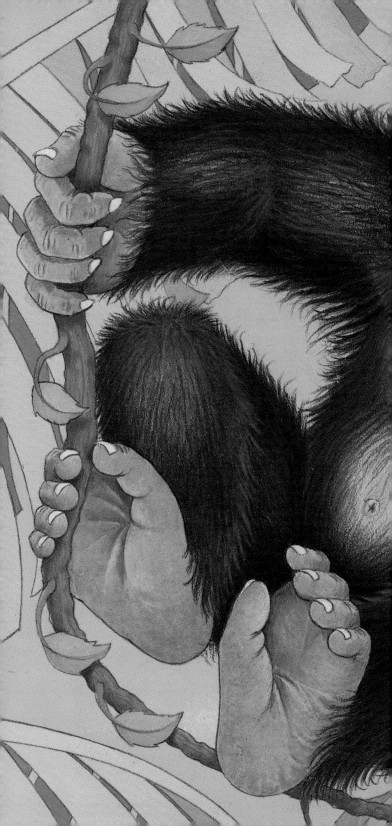

The monkey!

Who's lurking
in the swamp?
Watch out! It's ...

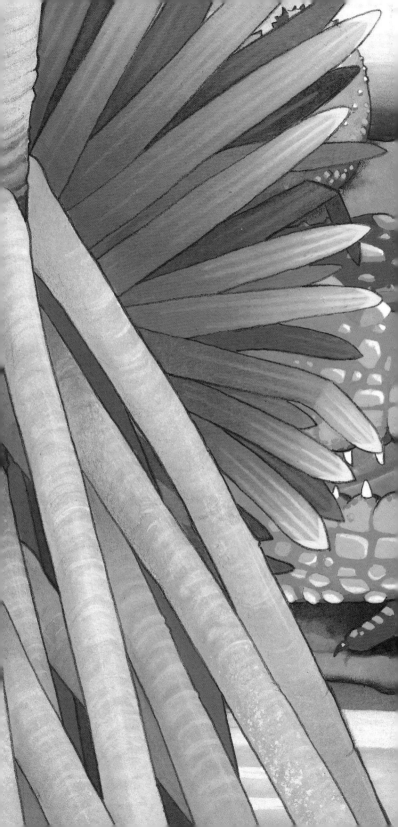

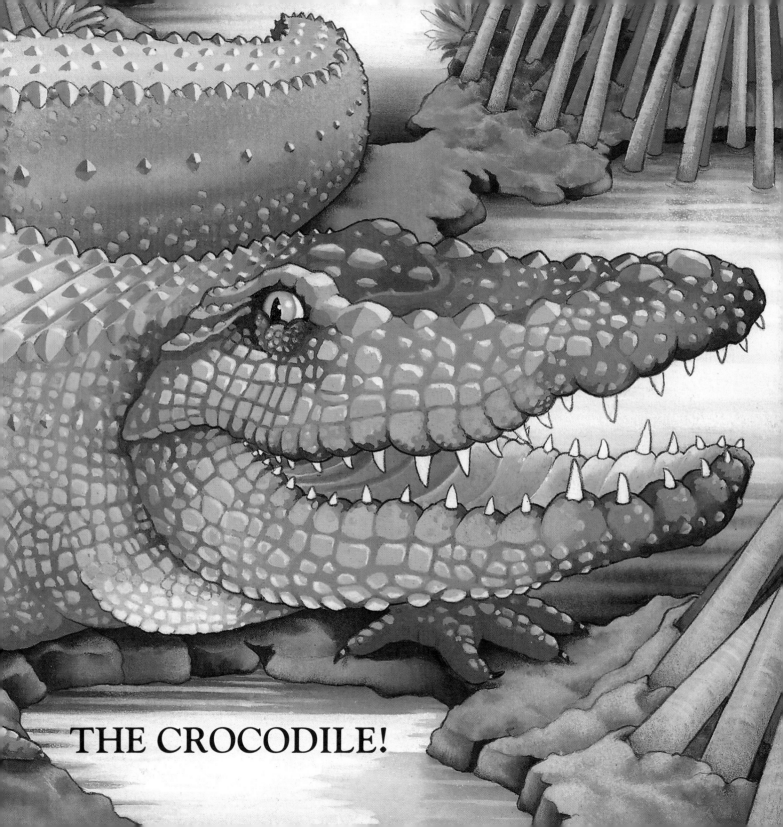

THE CROCODILE!

MORE WALKER PAPERBACKS
For You to Enjoy

Some more Flip-Flap Books

WHO'S ON THE FARM?
by Naomi Russell

Who's waiting by the gate? Who's rolling in the mud?
Who's splashing in the stream? Flip the flaps and see!

0-7445-6315-1   £3.99

RUNAWAY RABBIT
by Ron Maris

Rabbit is out of his hutch and running. But where will he go to?
Who will he see? Will he get away? Flip the flaps and see!

0-7445-6357-7   £3.99

WHERE'S MY EGG?
by Tony Mitton/Jane Chapman

Hen has lost her egg. Is it in Ben's kennel or Puss's bed or Donkey's straw?
Where can it be? Flip the flaps and see!

0-7445-6312-7   £3.99